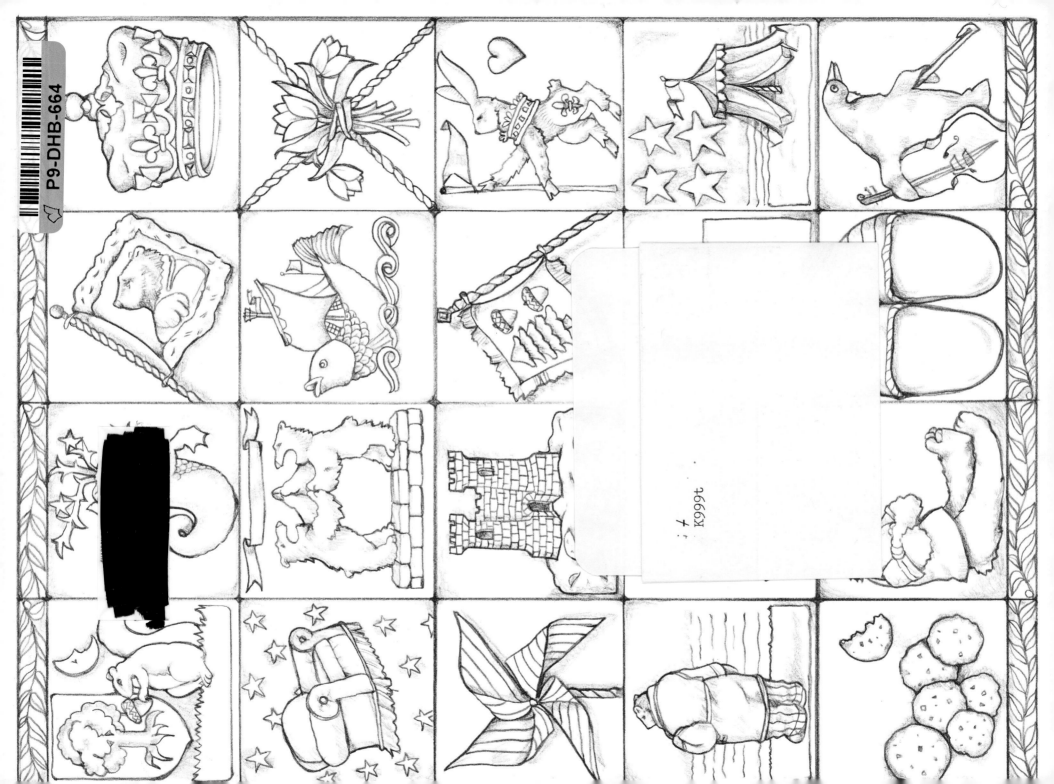

For All the Bears
Who Came Before

With special thanks to
Seymour Surnow

Copyright © 1985 by Dennis Kyte

All rights reserved
including the right of reproduction
in whole or in part in any form
Published by LITTLE SIMON
A Division of Simon & Schuster, Inc.
Simon & Schuster Building
Rockefeller Center
1230 Avenue of the Americas
New York, New York 10020
LITTLE SIMON and colophon are trademarks of Simon & Schuster, Inc.
Manufactured in the United States of America

1 2 3 4 5 6 7 8 9 10

Library of Congress Cataloging-in-Publication Data

Kyte, Dennis, 1947– To the heart of a bear.

Summary: A household of bears awakes early from hibernation to go on an amazing voyage
of discovery across ocean, desert, and mountain.
[1. Bears—Fiction. 2. Adventure and adventurers—Fiction] I. Title.
PZ7.K993To   1985   [Fic]   85-18217
ISBN 0-671-54781-X

Abiner Smoothie's Journey

To the Heart Of a Bear

Dennis Kyte

Little Simon

Published by Simon & Schuster, Inc., New York

The turrets and towers of Pipchippin-on-the-Harley were heavy with snow. The winter night was bright with moonlight. A single light shone in the library downstairs. Elsewhere in the house, Abiner Smoothie, quite out of character, was awake.

"Everyone else is asleep," Abiner growled, wandering down to the library. Knowing that Puppy is a rabbit who practically lives in the library, Abiner was not surprised to find him there poring over Spinoza. Puppy peered briefly over his spectacles and returned to his reading.

Standing there, rather at a loss as to what to do, Abiner found his gaze rising to the shrouded statue of the Bear in Disgrace.

High atop a marble column stood a clumsy-shaped thing covered in tapestry and tied tightly with silk-corded rope. Bears are kindly, and the idea that someone would do a dastardly deed was just too much to think about, so they didn't. Someone wisely covered the statue, and the Smoothie clan ignored it for centuries. No one for generations had dared to peek.

"Hmmmmm," he whispered to himself. "I've wondered who was under there since I was a cub."

Moving quietly toward the column that supported the bust, Abiner loosened the ancient silk cord and let it fall to the floor. Then, holding his breath and squinting his eyes, he pulled away the heavy tapestry—and lo and behold, Abiner came face-to-face with his forebear, the secretive Lady Audrey Furwhistle.

"I wonder how she disgraced our family, Puppy."

"She certainly was a beauty!" Puppy exclaimed, joining Abiner before the bear bust. "Just look at that ruby heart. And look here," Puppy went on, becoming quite excited, "under the necklace there is a verse chiseled in a fold in her dress."

Having read it, it didn't take Abiner a minute to know what to do. "Puppy, pack your things. I'm going to wake up the rest of the household."

"Whatever for?" asked Puppy.

"Read the verse, Pup, and you'll understand."

Whosoever lifts this drape and reveals my face
Will take a voyage through time and space
To search for the whole and not just the part;
For at journey's end, find the memory's heart.

Once roused, the household packed in a jiffy. In addition to Abner and Puppy, there were Abner's relatives, Galeazza Von Boyage (professional beauty and founder of the Folies Beargère), Lady Savoy "Squeezy" Beauchamp (darling, dim, and dithering widow of Lord Beauchamp), and dotty old Seaton Willoughby. (Seaton was well known as the author of mystery stories and forest whodunits. His most recent, *The Topiary Murders*, had received wide acclaim, good reviews, and even some threatening mail from outraged gardeners.)

Abiner took charge of the expedition. Everyone was outfitted, looking swell. Seaton had even brought along Dr. Gladstone, his dog with spots. The group chattered and carried on excitedly, except for Galeazza, who was just a little grumpy about being awakened before April.

Abiner made sure that everything, especially the ruby heart, was safely tucked in his bags. The footmen, Fizdale and Crimmins, helped everyone into the coach. After a bit of arguing about the seating, they all settled down for the two days it took to get to the ocean.

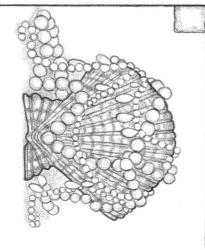

The sojourn to the ocean was a jolly one. Afternoons were spent playing Whist and Count the Cows and feasting on mounds of watercress sandwiches, spicy meat tarts and cookies for Afters.

The sun was just setting as they arrived at the harbor where the *Argyle* was docked. That night they all settled down in their cabins for a good night's sleep, awakening to find they were already at sea.

Hurrying to breakfast, everyone took his or her usual place at the table. Napkins under chins, they waited patiently. There was not a sound from the galley. The hungry group waited and waited. Suddenly from the galley came the sound of pots and pans banging, plates breaking, squeals, and even some gutteral utterances. Abiner looked alarmed. "Whatever can be the matter?" he asked.

"Don't worry, darling!" Squeezy whispered, so that no one else could hear. "Captain Finnegan told me that Chef Rudy is a genius in the kitchen. He's cordon bleu."

"Well," said Abiner matter-of-factly, "he is making too much noise, whatever color his coat is." The noisy racket from the galley came to a crashing halt.

Everyone looked to the galley doors. There was a long pause as the group waited until the galley doors flew open and six waiters brought each breakfaster a covered plate. Everyone gasped as the lids were lifted, and each stared at the revealed meal. Chef Rudy had celebrated the first morning at sea with "Omelet Portraits." Each eggy likeness was a perfect caricature. Puppy said that Rudy's dual talents were tasty as well as flattering. All agreed, except Galleazza, who complained that he had made her ears too large and that green pepper pieces did not in the least look like emeralds.

Breakfast was interrupted as a gam of porpoises surrounded the *Argyle*, swaying in the foam and singing in gurgles and beeps. Just when Abiner and Puppy left the table to get a closer look, one of the finny creatures rose up on the slippery backs of the others and gave Abiner a beautiful seashell. With a splash, the porpoises disappeared into the brine as quickly as they had appeared, as though into a dream. On closer inspection of the shell, Abiner said, "Pup, there's a bit of writing here on the underside. Listen."

A tiny boat is waiting to take you away
Where mermaids lead sea stags to Silver Moon Cay,
With armfuls of cakes and ices and flowers,
They whisper you welcome to undersea towers.

Even the most skeptical breakfaster had to believe them then.

the bottom of the sea," he said.

adventure until Abiner produced a beautifully carved fish. "This comes from a castle at

At breakfast next morning, no one believed the story of their midnight underwater

Abiner and Puppy climbed aboard, and with a swash and a giggle, they were off.

A host of mermaids appeared to them, with sea stags who were pulling a boat.

and Puppy waited on deck in the moonlight.

anchor and each bunk had a bear snoring away, Abiner

And so it was that at midnight, as the Argyle lay at

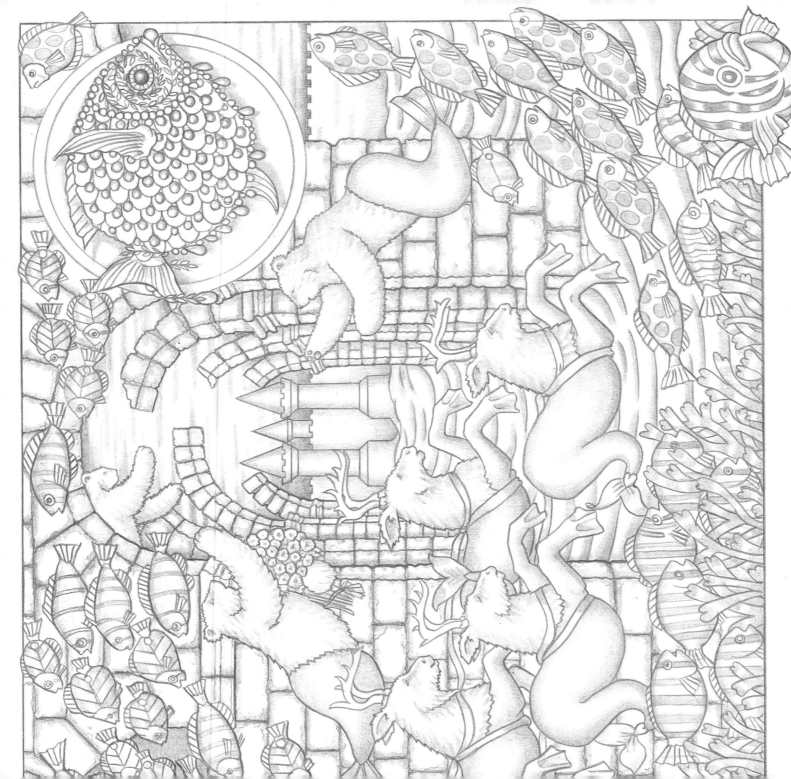

Seaton begged to have a closer look at the fish. After putting on his spectacles he said, "Did you two chaps happen to notice that each scale has a letter carved into it?" He continued, "I believe I can just make it out."

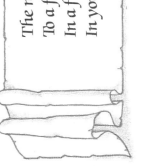

The next time to travel, you cross yellow yellow sands
To a forest of palms, where one palm understands.
In a fine golden nest, an egg blushes pink;
In your search for the chain, this is a link.

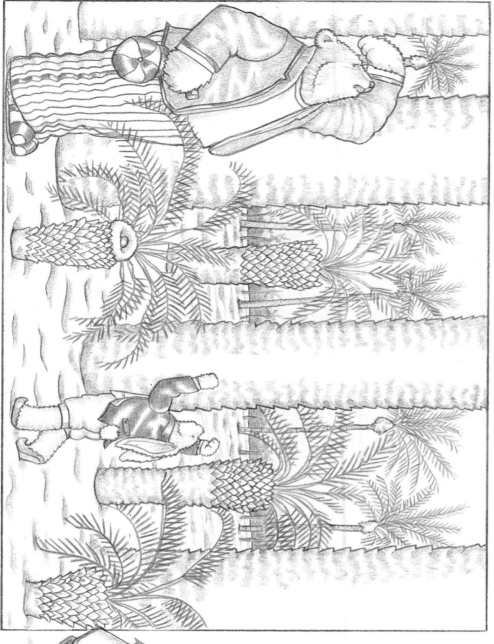

Abiner immediately ordered the ship's course changed. Just as the scaly missive had told them to do, they soon docked, trading their ship of the ocean for those of the desert.

On camelback, they rode across endless sands until they came to a forest of palmettos. Nestled in the smallest palmetto was a golden nest, and in it was a single pink egg. Turning it over and over, Abiner searched in vain for a message.

The ursine explorers moved on, until they came to a desert kingdom and a castle rising high into the sky. There, singing torchbearers and veiled maidens escorted them up the winding path to the legendary Castle Muchadew.

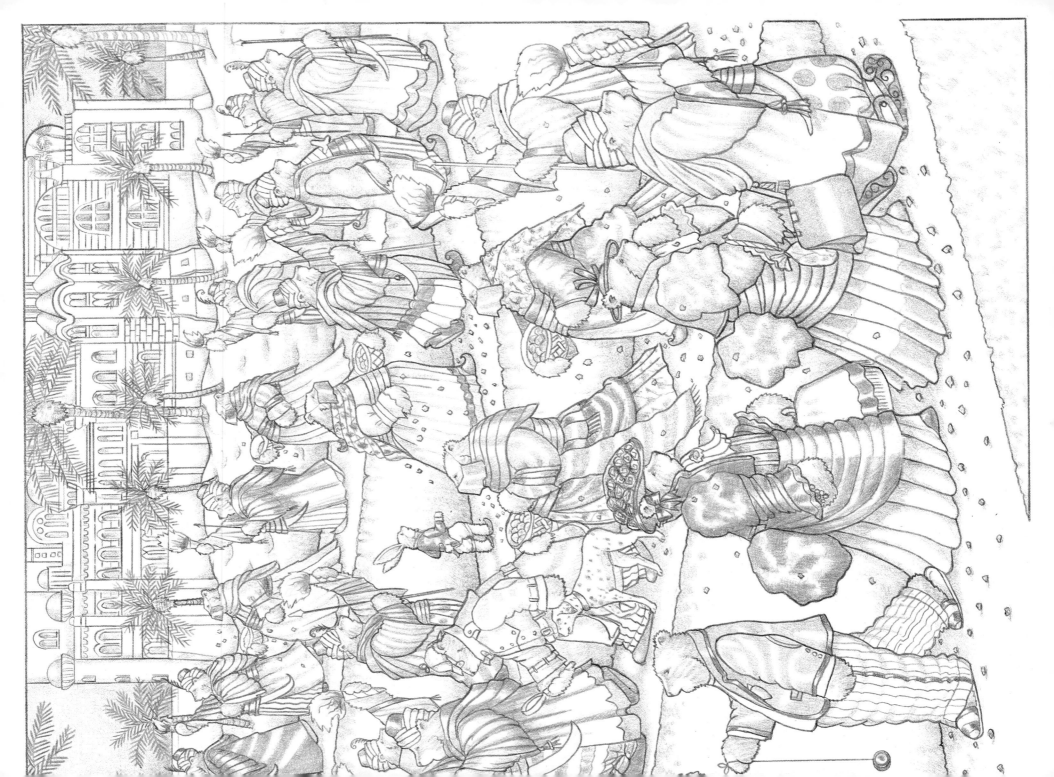

That evening they were feted by the Grand Wazir. After a sumptuous meal of nettle leaves, hibiscus shoots, and honey-flavored concoctions, the potentate delighted his guests with an

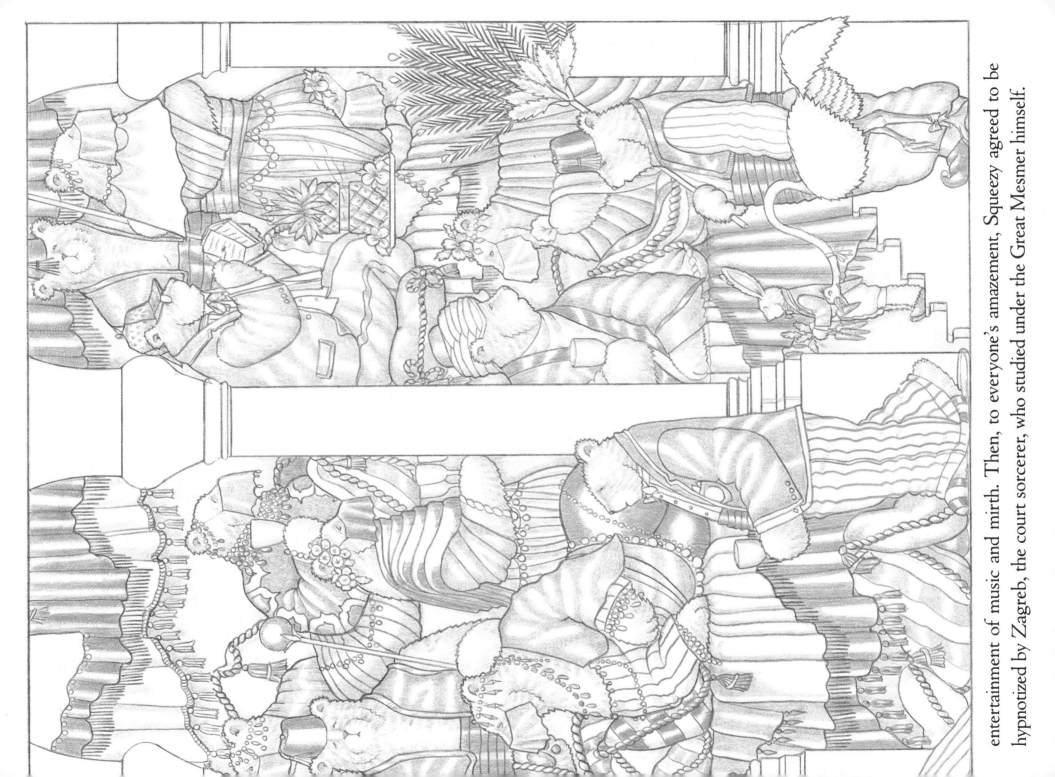

entertainment of music and mirth. Then, to everyone's amazement, Squeezy agreed to be hypnotized by Zagreb, the court sorcerer, who studied under the Great Mesmer himself.

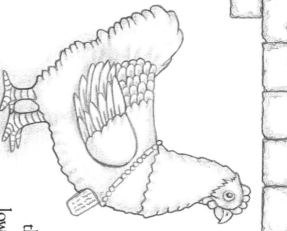

The next morning, after a breakfast of pineapple porridge, the Wazir took Abiner's arm and said, "Smoothie, before you leave, I must show you something very special."

Abiner was delighted at such a royal honor. The two bears proceeded to a part of the castle known only to the Wazir. They came to a wall in which there was a tiny red door. Crawling on all fours, Abiner followed the potentate through the door into a secret chamber. There they sat on pillows around a table on which sat a silver chicken surrounded by eggs shaped from jewels of every color—except pink. Abiner reached into his pocket for the egg he had found in the tiny palmetto.

"Your Highness has been so kind to us. May I present you with this egg?"

"A pink egg, my dear Smoothie!" the Wazir exclaimed. "You have completed my collection of eggs. This is most generous of you! In exchange, you must accept this silver chicken, which has magical powers that can unlock mysteries."

Abiner made a bow and said thank you. He took the chicken but showed it to no one. The voyagers said their good-byes and set off on camelback across the desert. They traveled the rest of the day and night, for the chicken with the gold tag around its neck told Abiner they must.

The bears came upon a forest. There a young cub, who seemed to be waiting for them, held four white horses.

Abiner exchanged his camel for a horse. The others did the same and, clanking the young groom, they headed down the grassy path single file.

They had gone only a short distance when Dr. Gladstone announced that he heard a commotion up ahead. And indeed, when they crossed a tree-covered bridge, there in the valley below was a wondrous celebration in full swing.

This is surely what the chicken foretold, Abiner said. Clearing his throat, he recited the verse aloud for all to hear.

Follow a course through a tree-tunnel bright;
Cross a bridge to a world where Day is Knight.
This time is neither your master nor mistress,
But secrets are kept by damsels in distress.

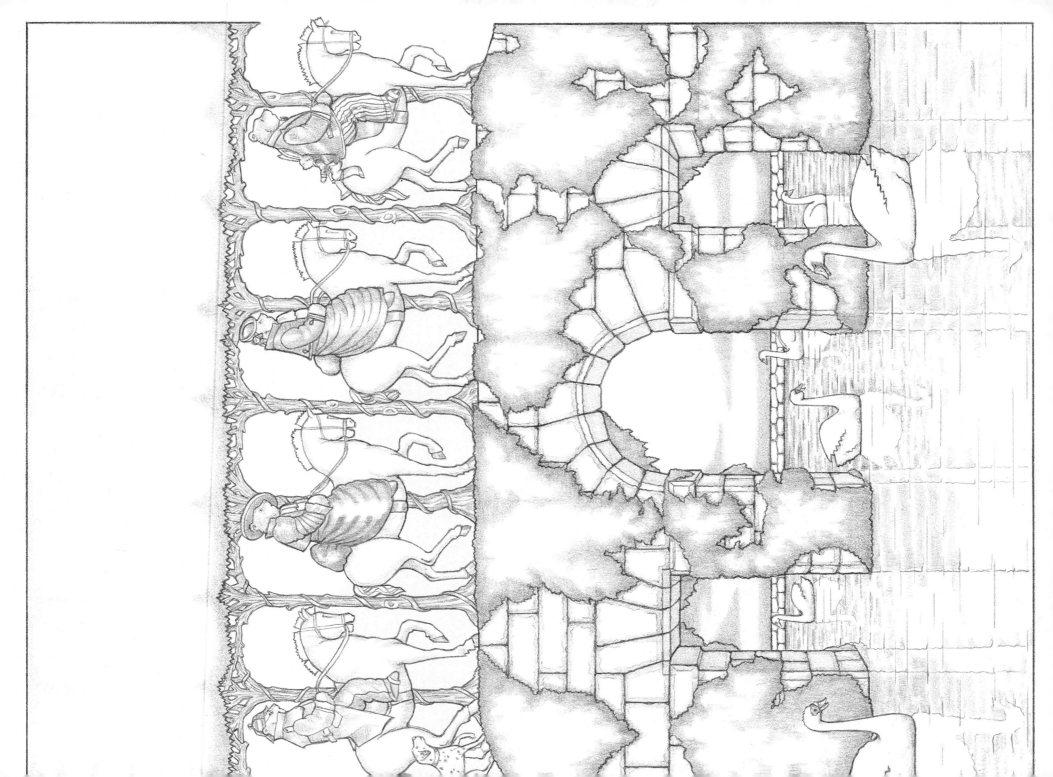

"Oh, a picnic with jousting. How daring!" Galeazza cried as she led the way down into the valley. After lunch Abiner

Everyone agreed to join the revelry. After lunch Abiner noticed a knight sitting off by himself.

"I am Abiner Smoothie," he said cheerfully. In the saddest voice that Abiner had ever heard, the knight looked up and replied, "I am Sir Day."

Abiner learned that Sir Day was sad because his lady love had been bewitched by an evil

sorceress. The unfortunate damsel was trapped in a tree, and try though he may, Sir Day could not free her.

"How dreadful," Abiner said. "My friend Puppy and I shall help you rescue her."

"Even the forest philosophers have failed," Sir Day lamented.

"Stuff and nonsense," Abiner said firmly, and in no time the three set out into the forest.

And rescue the damsel is just what they did. Sir Day led them into the darkest depths of the forest where they were surrounded by huge trees. There were elms and ash, spruce and pine, growing so closely together the travelers were forced to walk a particular path. Their trek was slowed by the knee-deep fern and flora that was the forest floor.

"Abiner," Puppy said, "have you noticed the forest is laid out like a puzzle? How will we ever find Sir Day's maiden?" Just then, along with the wind blowing through the trees, was the faint sound of someone crying.

"Listen!" Abiner said. The three stopped in their tracks, listened, and heard the crying again.

"Oh dear, oh dear, oh dear!" Sir Day cried. "It's so sad."

"Don't worry," Puppy said, pointing over his head. "I think we have found her." And sure enough, towering over them were two giant twin oaks. Abiner circled one of the trees, growling to himself. He rubbed his paws over the tree, looking for something. Finally with a confused look on his face, he said to Puppy and Sir Day, "Must be barking up the wrong tree."

Abiner circled the other tree round and round. Locating a small indentation in the bark, Abiner searched his pocket for the silver chicken the Wazir had given him. Placing it in the tree bark, he turned it like a key. Magically, the ancient tree groaned and began to shrink away until it dissolved into the air. Sir Day fell to his knees. In only a moment, the tree—in fact, the entire forest maze—was no more. In its place stood a beautiful damsel, holding a blue crystal acorn with a teardrop inside.

"The forest was just an illusion to protect one tree," Abiner said to himself.

After the damsel and knight embraced, she turned to Abiner and whispered, "Before you take your leave, kind sir, I have a secret to impart." And without speaking another word, the maiden pressed the tear-filled acorn into his paw. It was inscribed with this verse.

Bid farewell the forest and look to the skies;
In mountaintop shadows the real truth lies.
Wherever you wander, there you will find
That the path to the heart is all in the mind.

The lovers were reunited. The sojourners bade them farewell beneath a sky orange with butterflies. It took them weeks to reach the top of the mountain.

One evening they came upon a woman selling Cupids.

On their climb, they met the dancing sisters, Joy and Abandon.

At last the travelers came upon the Three-Pillared Gate of Wisdom.

Perhaps the most startling sight was that of Crime being pursued by Justice and Vengeance.

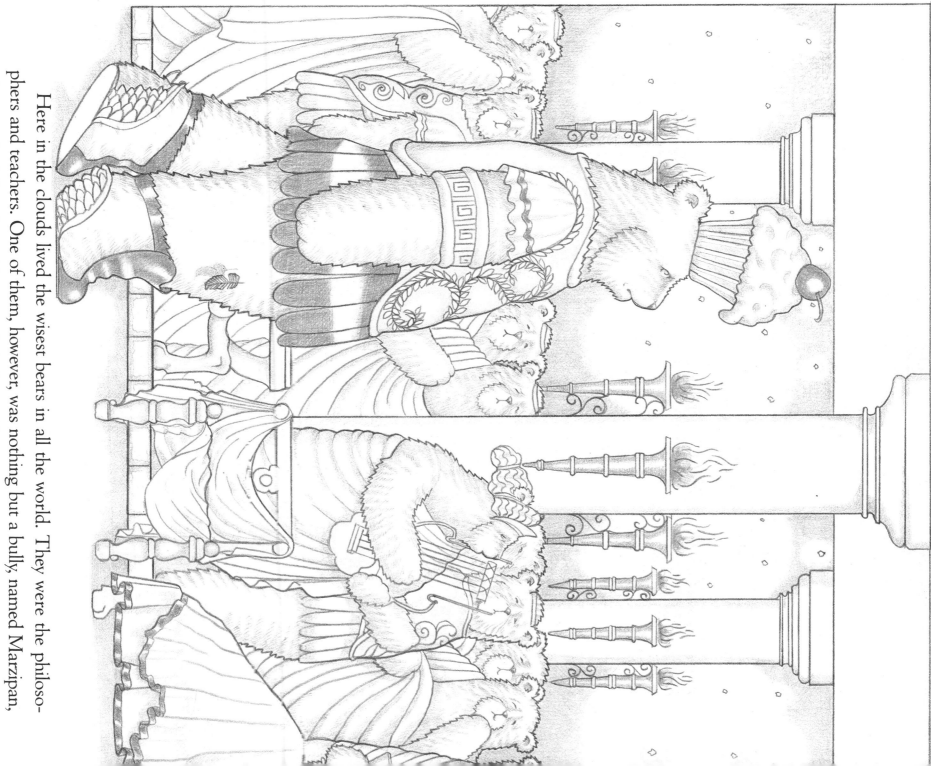

Here in the clouds lived the wisest bears in all the world. They were the philosophers and teachers. One of them, however, was nothing but a bully, named Marzipan, who marched directly to Abiner and challenged him to a Funny-Hat Duel.

"Oh dread!" the philosophers cried in chorus.

But that night Abiner surprised everyone by winning the duel paws down. They all

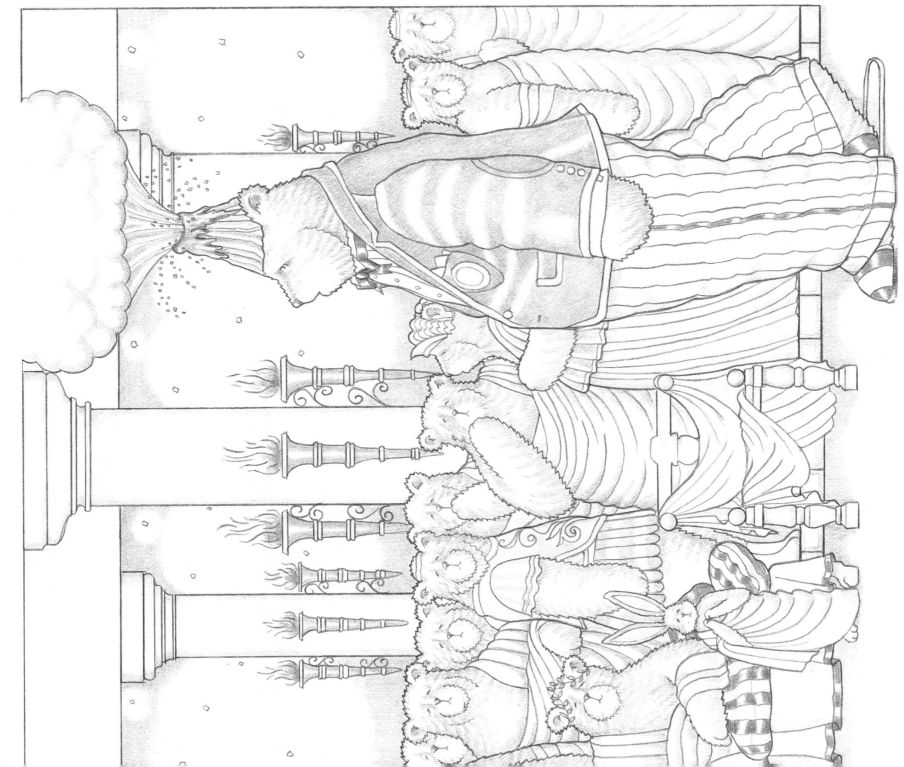

cheered as Abiner's volcano hat sputtered and spewed lava carefully concocted of raspberry jam. Even Marzipan had to doff his cupcake cap before Abiner's splendid *chapeau disastre*.

"How nice," Puppy whispered to the wise philosopher Bear Cloudius, "to save the day with a natural disaster."

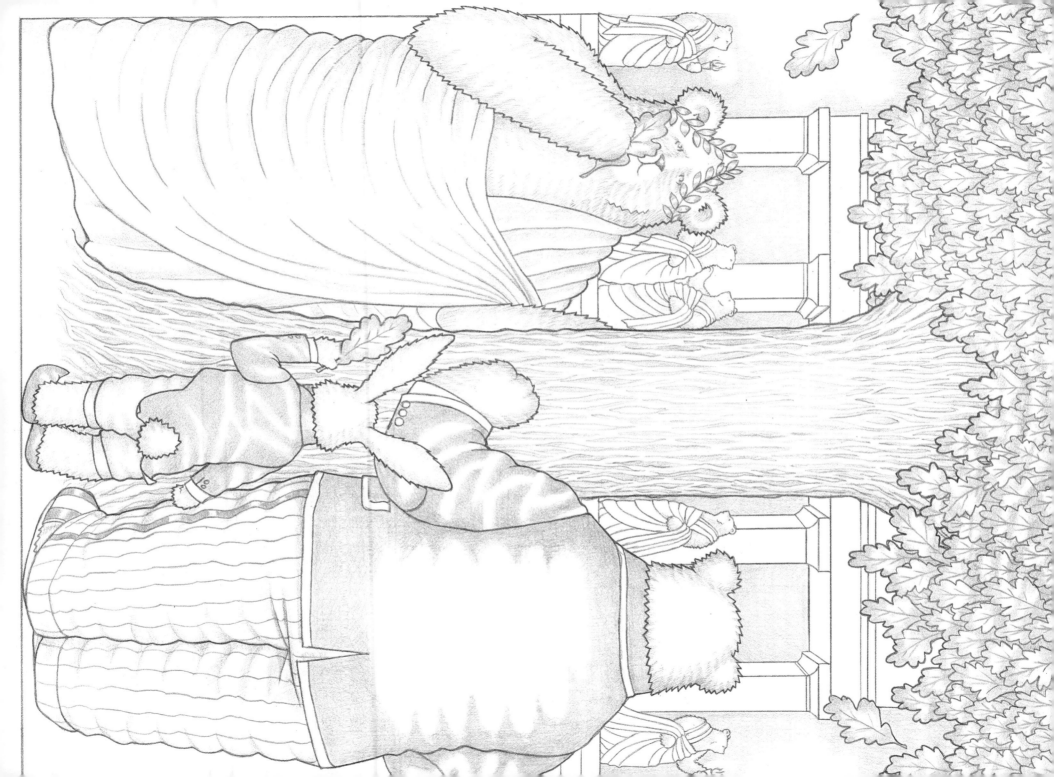

A week later, Abiner was walking with Bear Cloudius, the oldest and wisest of all the great bear thinkers. Abiner remarked on the beauty of his mountaintop home. Bear Cloudius smiled and said, "There is only one wish that cannot be fulfilled here in the clouds."

It did not take Abiner long to learn that what Bear Cloudius longed for was a tree. Abiner held up the crystal acorn and exclaimed, "Let us plant this in a clearing away from the mountain's shadow."

There was barely time to pat the ground when there came a rumbling beneath their feet. Before Bear Cloudius's amazed eyes grew an oak of monumental proportion. His eyes filled with grateful tears as he thanked Abiner repeatedly.

That twilight saw Abiner and company preparing to depart. The philosophers gathered to say good-bye and give remembrances. Grandest of all was the ancient bear relic Bear Cloudius gave Abiner to thank him for his generosity. "This is our most valued treasure," said Bear Cloudius, handing Abiner an urn.

"What do these pictures on it mean?" Puppy wanted to know.

"They illustrate a verse we have studied for years, but no one can understand what it means."

Abiner told the kind old gentleman that he could not accept so valued a relic but would accept the verse with pleasure.

There is a web that the blue sea weaves;
A story is told in chrysanthemum leaves.
The secret that a snowflake made
Is held by an emperor made of jade.

After leaving the philosophers, they headed back down to the sea. Galeazza and Squeezy were in charge of the theatricals, songfests, and theme parties. One night Galeazza dressed up as a fortune teller and conducted a seance complete with a spirit from the other world.

Probably the most fun was celebrating Puppy's birthday. Chef Rudy made a special cake and birthday chair.

The air was fragrant with flowers as the Argyle dropped anchor.

The "Least Favorite Kings" costume gala was great fun—everyone dressed as the monarch he or she liked least.

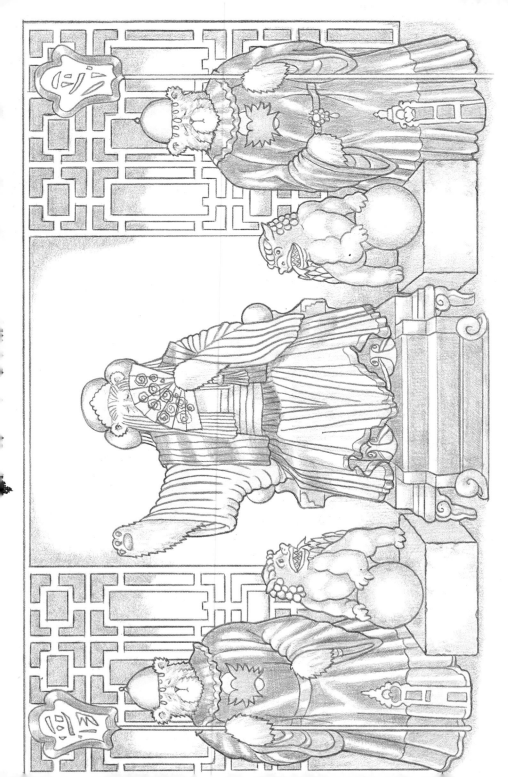

The entire group squeezed into a dinghy and rowed ashore. When they arrived at the Imperial Palace, the guards seemed to be expecting them.

Abiner, Puppy, and friends were brought into a grand chamber where they set eyes on the beautiful principessa. She asked Abiner what had brought his party here. Abiner explained his quest for the heart of the bear and was surprised to learn that the principessa too was searching for a heart.

"You see, many centuries ago a galleon arrived at our shores from the Fililli Islands. The lovely Lady Audrey Furwhistle was aboard. These visitors seemed to come in friendship. We did not know that she was an infamous pirate queen who sailed the seas with an eye to steal the world's most coveted jewels. When they left, we discovered they had taken my great grandmother's most treasured posession, a necklace with an enormous ruby heart. This necklace has magical powers for us, and without it, a principessa cannot love."

Abiner rushed to his bag and returned with the ruby heart, presenting it to the principessa in a small leather sack.

"Your heart," Abiner said gallantly.

The courtiers fell silent as the grateful potentate held the heart. She looked at Abiner and smiled.

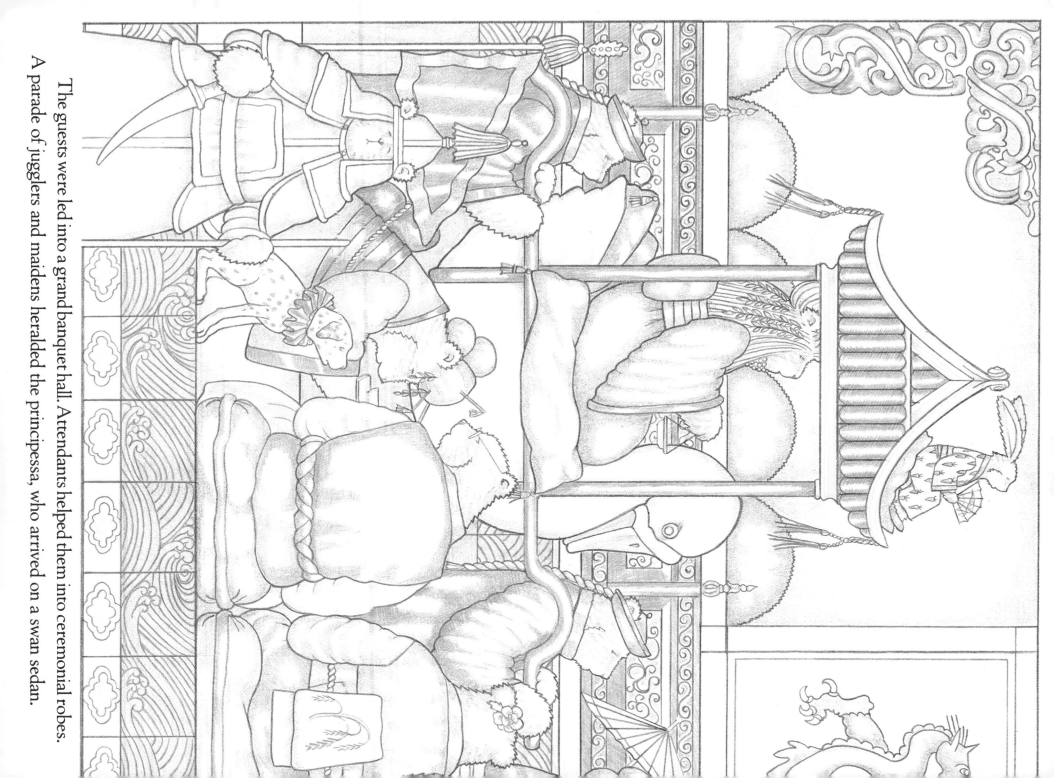

The guests were led into a grand banquet hall. Attendants helped them into ceremonial robes. A parade of jugglers and maidens heralded the principessa, who arrived on a swan sedan.

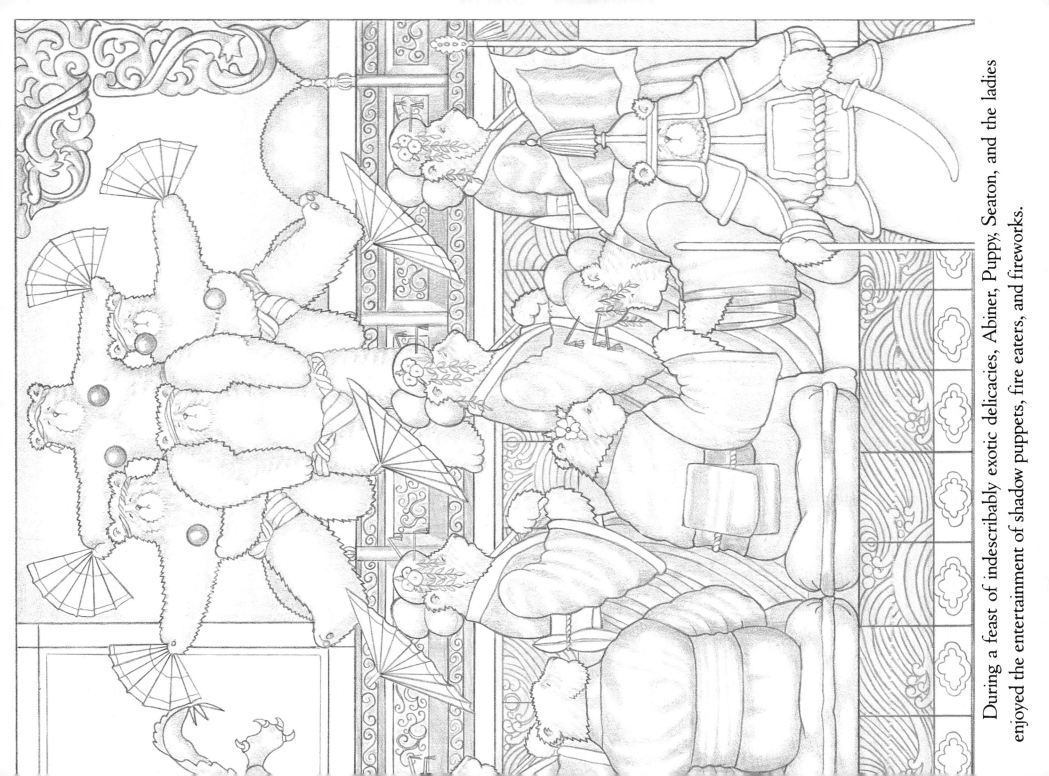

During a feast of indescribably exotic delicacies, Abiner, Puppy, Seaton, and the ladies enjoyed the entertainment of shadow puppets, fire eaters, and fireworks.

After dinner, the group were shown to their bed-chambers. Serenaded by harp players, everyone slept pleasantly. Abiner awoke to the sound of gentle tapping at his chamber door. To his surprise, the principessa herself had come to invite him to stroll with her in the palace gardens. They came upon a quiet bench where chrysanthemums and roses intertwined to make an arbor.

"You have given me back my heart," the principessa said, "and now I know the joy of love."

Abiner was very pleased until he realized that it was he, in fact, who was the object of the principessa's affection. She asked Abiner to stay with her forever, sharing her palace, wealth, and chamber.

It would be unfair to say that Abiner was not tempted, but he answered resolutely that he must continue his quest.

The principessa, in a manner befitting her royal station, accepted Abiner's decision with dignity and even helped him make ready for his departure. As a farewell gesture, she handed Abiner a jade statue of a warrior emperor fitted with gold.

"This is the emperor in the philosopher's verse," Abiner declared. The statue held a round package wrapped in a piece of silk.

Abiner laid aside the silk wrapping and found a small globe in the center of which was trapped one perfect snowflake. Woven into the silk wrapping were the following words:

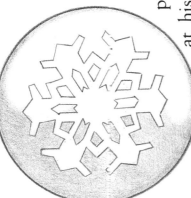

The next truth is buried under deep snow;
To learn that secret is the way to know,
The path going backward is really the start,
For the center of all things is truly the heart.

"Where are we off to now, Smoothie?" Seaton asked when they returned to the ship.

"Due north!" Abiner replied. "The North Pole, I think."

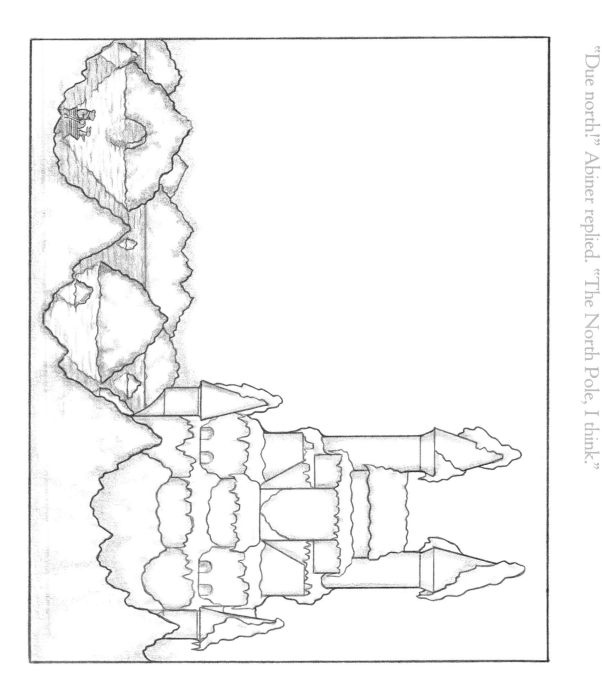

After sailing north for two months, everyone awoke one morning to the surprise of cold. Bits of ice floated in the sea. The *Argyle* sailed past Penguin Island, through the Bay of Frigia and up a narrow river where the crew spied an island. On the island was a palace made entirely out of ice and shrouded in mist. The *Argyle* came to rest in the harbor. All around them was an eerie silence. And the stillness only made it seem colder.

The captain, crew, Seaton, and the ladies excused themselves as Abiner and Puppy dressed in furs and took the dinghy ashore. They tied up at a frozen dock and made their way up to the gate of the palace, reassuring each other the whole way.

The castle's huge doors stood open. Abiner and Puppy walked in and suddenly saw why everything was so still. Before their eyes sat the king and queen, frozen on their thrones. Confronted with this vision, Abiner could say nothing.

Puppy whispered, "Did you bring the snowflake with you?"

Abiner nodded yes, and handed the snowflake to Puppy, who unwrapped it and walked carefully to the thrones. Abiner followed reluctantly.

Puppy approached the little bridge that separated the thrones of the king and queen, noticing a pattern of snowflakes and a small hole in the center. Puppy slipped the globed snowflake into the hole.

The ice began to crack. One crack followed another, then another. Suddenly the glassy veneer covering everything began to crack and fall away. The sound of dripping water could be heard everywhere.

The king came alive. He stood and kissed the hand of his queen and then turned to the visitors and said, "You have saved us from a terrible fate! During our wedding ceremony, a wicked fairy put a curse on us. She was jealous of our love, so she froze my kingdom, thinking it would freeze my heart. But during the hundreds of years I have waited in this icy prison, my love has only grown stronger."

And so Abiner and Puppy joined in the festivities as the wedding ceremony resumed where it had left off.

They returned to the ship carrying a present wrapped with colored string and bearing a tag that said "Thank you."

"Open it, Abiner," Puppy said. Inside was a long leather box, tooled in gold. Abiner opened the box and found a bottle. He removed the stopper and the smell of jasmine and spices filled the air.

Before them in a puff of smoke appeared an enormous genie. Our heroes might not have believed their eyes except that they distinctly heard the genie utter these words:

You'll find that the step that fills the space
Proves that the heart is a cavernous place.
And though small, the strength it holds in its core
Is the treasure of all that has come before.

The ship got under way as soon as Abiner and Puppy were back aboard. How pleasant it was as they once again sailed into warmer climes south past Cape Tulip and through the straits of Frondadieu until they reached the Island of Balibonia. Here, according to the map, a sharp left would, in three months' time, put them at their destination. The voyage was long, but fair weather and congenial company made the time fly by. Land was sighted in late September. The explorers, well rested, eagerly went ashore

and set about the rigors of following both their map and verse through forest and fjord until, crossing a mountain, they found themselves standing in a valley that time seemed to have forgotten. Past herds of grazing dinosaurs and dens of friendly cave bears, they journeyed on until at last they reached a cave.

Into the mouth of the cave was carved the fierce shape of a bear's head. And it was at the head of this bear that our travelers made their camp.

The next morning, what with Seaton writing in his journal and Squeezy, Galeazza, and Dr. Gladstone dressing up the dinosaurs with bows, Abiner Smoothie and Puppy ventured into the cave alone, bearing torches.

Just when they were both privately thinking they had gone astray, they came up to a huge, faded drawing on one wall of the cave. They lit another torch and on closer

inspection, they agreed it was a picture of a goat with a pineapple. They continued deeper into the cave and soon they saw more drawings of birds and fishes and horses and monkeys and a giraffe, until at last they came to what they both knew they had been seeking these many months.

It was a bear.

The very first bear.

"Say, Pup," Abiner said as he held the torch closer to the painting. "It looks like me."

Puppy nodded. "There is no mistaking the likeness." Then he became quite excited. "What's this?" he asked.

Abiner moved the torch a bit higher. In the warm firelight there was no mistaking this likeness either—long ears, bright green eyes, and that tiny face, peering out from behind the hulking figure of the bear on the wall.

To the side of the painting, Abiner and Puppy together read the final verse.

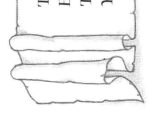

The end of your journey lies here at the source;
Ends are beginnings when good deeds guide your course.
The last and the first are not far apart;
You will find your way home if you follow your heart.

The turrets and towers of Pipchippin were heavy with snow. The winter night was bright with moonlight. Only a light in the library showed any signs of life in the great house on the Harley.

Abiner opened the doors to the library and saw Puppy reading Spinoza.

"You're up early," Puppy said.

Abiner stared at him for a moment. "Puppy, I've had the most astonishing dream."

"No, Puppy, you don't understand! I've found it! I've found the heart of the bear!"

"Have you really? Good," said Puppy, going back to his book.

"Quite so," Abiner said as he turned to leave.

"Smooth sailing, Smoothie. Go back to sleep."

"Yes, sleep," said Abiner, yawning until his eyes watered. "It's been quite...some... night."

As Puppy listened to Abiner's slippered footfalls scuffle down the hall to bed, he quietly sang the bedtime song to himself.

Hum de dum, blanket and pillow,
My bed's a sailboat with sheets all a-billow.
My animals are crew; my signal's a yawn!
We sail after midnight, but home before dawn.

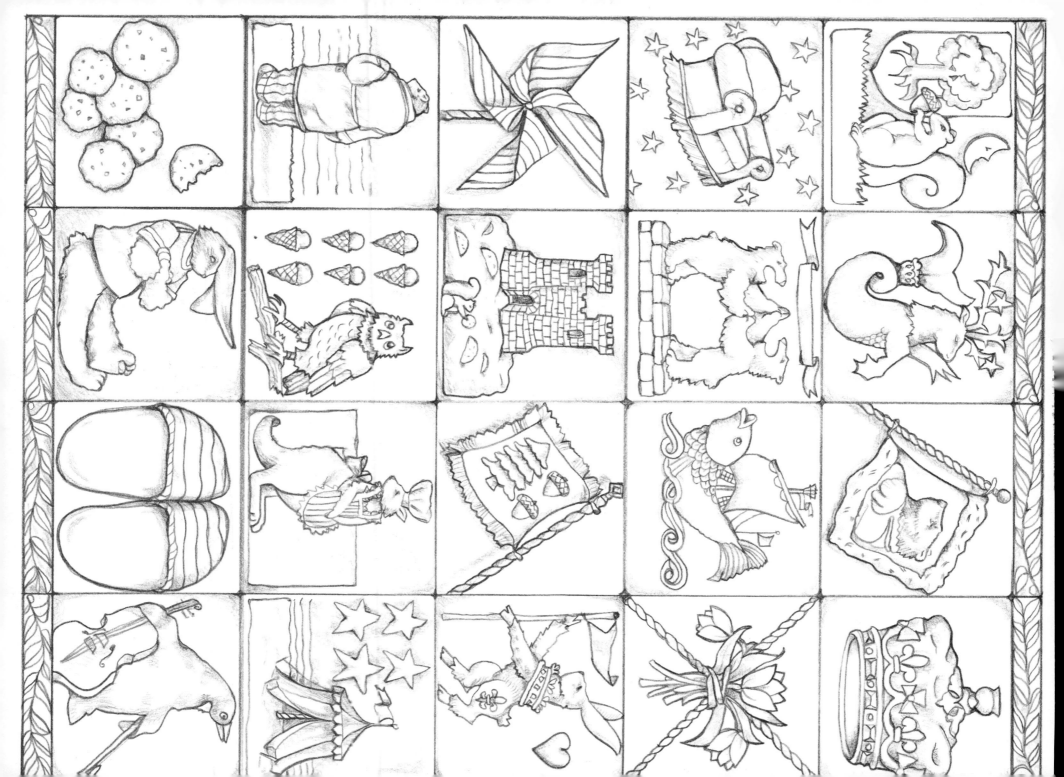